DERBY DOWNS

by
Stephen Cosgrove
Illustrated by
Wendy Edelson

MULTNOMAH

10209 SE Division Street, Portland, Oregon 97266

Library of Congress Cataloging-in Publication Data

Cosgrove, Stephen.
    Derby Downs.

    Summary: Derby Downs persuades the other young
bunnies to ignore the advice of the elder rabbits and start
building houses above ground, even though the wisdom
and experience of the oldsters suggests it is safer to remain
in the burrows underground..
    [1. Rabbits—Fiction. 2. Old age—Fiction.] I. Edelson,
Wendy, ill. II. Title
PZ7.C8117De 1988   [E]   88-25526

©1988 by Stephen Cosgrove
Published by Multnomah Press
Portland, Oregon 97266
Printed in USA
All Rights Reserved.
ISBN 0-88070-240-0

91 92 93 94 95 96 97 98 - 9 8 7 6 5 4 3 2

Dedicated to Sam Walton
as wise as the silvered hares
in the Land of Barely There.

Farther than far
and to the very edge of the horizon was a path bordered with lacy fern. If you walked down that path, following the dancing squirrels and singing birds, you would find a land called Barely There.

Barely There . . . a land where crickets sang as the sun went down and chipmunks danced in the light of the moon. A land where the summer night wind whispered gently through the trees, "Barely There! Barely There!" as the stars glistened in scented skies.

If, at dawn, you followed that winding path through the silvered pines, you would find a meadow brimming with life. Button Bow Roses and wild carrots grew in delightful profusion. Green bushy bushes dripping with blossoms called to the bumblebees buzzing in the air.

It was here in this magical meadow that the bunnies of Barely There lived and played their lives away. Big bunnies, little bunnies, old and new, hippled and hopped in the grasses that grew.

The bunnies lived below the meadow in warm, cozy burrows. The twisted tunnels laced beneath the meadow like a maze leading from one bunny's home to another.

Bits of root and vine lined the earthen walls where candles dripped the wax of ages. Though the cavelike tunnels were a bit damp, they served their purpose just fine, for they had been built like this for all of time by the older bunnies.

But the younger bunnies didn't like the tunnels. They thought the burrows were dark and dank. They yearned to live in the open skies of the meadows above.

One of the younger bunnies was called Derby Downs. He was neither young nor old. He was at a special age when all bunnies think they have learned all there is to learn. Derby was *sure* he knew all there was to know, and anything he didn't know wasn't worth knowing.

One day, as Derby and his grandfather, Samuel T., were walking in the meadow, Derby stopped, looked about and said, "You know, Grandpa Sam, I think it's time the bunnies moved up into the meadow."

"Eeeyup," said the silvered hare in his golden voice, "In the good old days, when I was a boy, I used to think the same thing. Even back then there was a silly young bunny who talked all the other bunnies into building above the ground. But there came mighty mountain storms that blew the meadow clean. That silly bunny learned that the burrows are better. Eeeyup, the burrows are better."

Derby laughed a knowing laugh, "Oh, Grandpa, when you were a boy there were dinosaurs. No, I think we'll build a new place to live above the ground in the meadow."

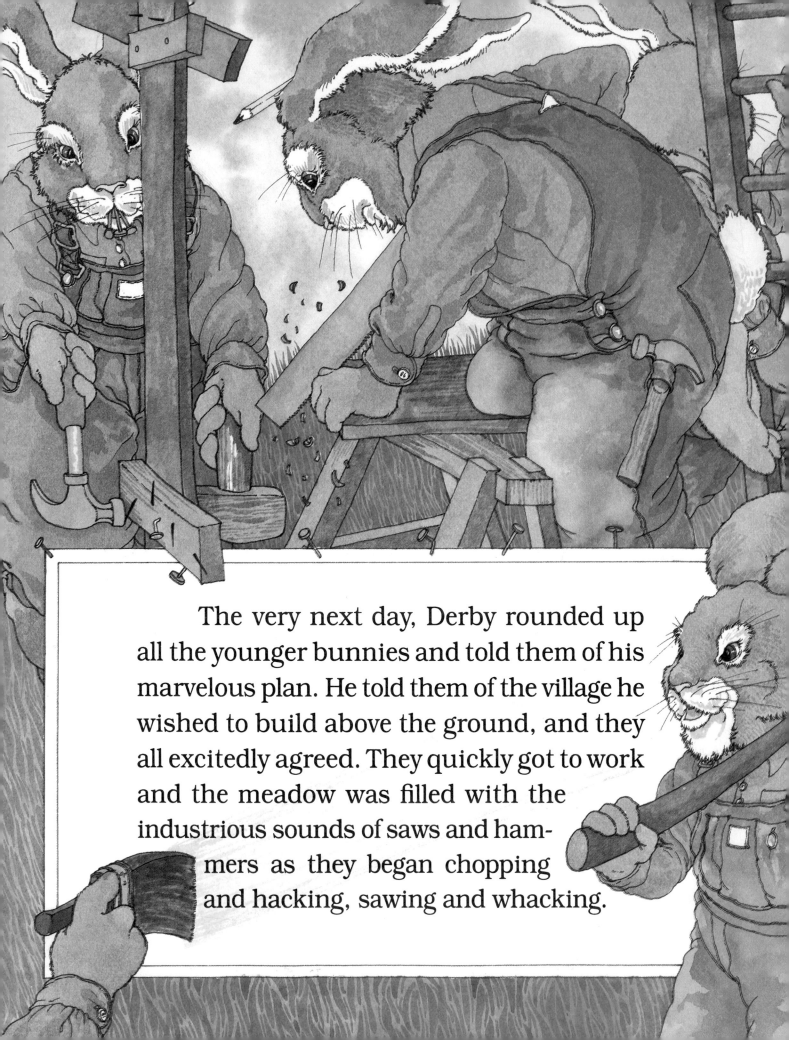

The very next day, Derby rounded up all the younger bunnies and told them of his marvelous plan. He told them of the village he wished to build above the ground, and they all excitedly agreed. They quickly got to work and the meadow was filled with the industrious sounds of saws and hammers as they began chopping and hacking, sawing and whacking.

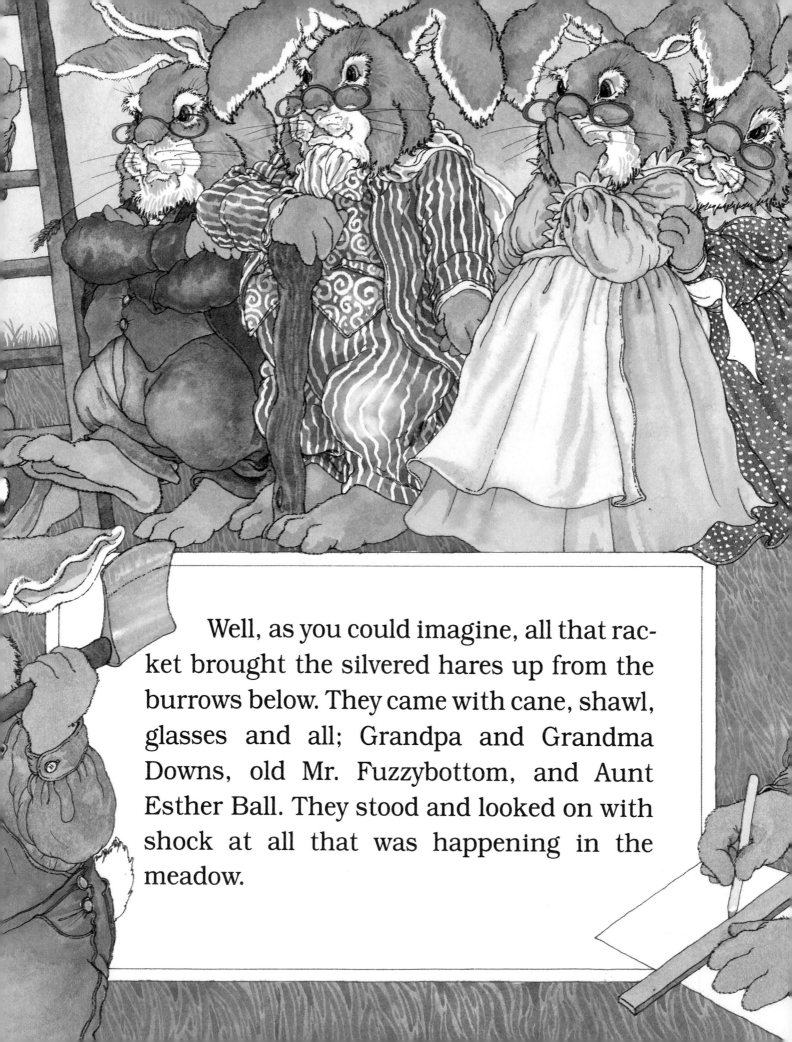

Well, as you could imagine, all that racket brought the silvered hares up from the burrows below. They came with cane, shawl, glasses and all; Grandpa and Grandma Downs, old Mr. Fuzzybottom, and Aunt Esther Ball. They stood and looked on with shock at all that was happening in the meadow.

The old rabbits watched, and finally old Grandpa Downs stepped forward and tapped Derby on the shoulder with his cane. "Stop this building immediately, young rabbits. For you are making an error great! When I was but a boy we had to live in the burrows for safety and warmth. There will come mighty mountain storms."

All the bunnies stopped their hammering and gathered about listening to the older ones. Then Derby spoke. "That was the olden days, Grandpa. Now is a time of youth and spring. No, we won't stop." With that Derby turned back to his work.

"But this is nonsense," said the older rabbit as he grabbed Derby's sleeve.

"Listen to me," said Derby as he shrugged off the old man and shouted to all the grayed ones, "You older rabbits are just in the way. Take a walk in the sunshine or go knit a blanket, but leave us be, for this is progress." And with that all the young rabbits went back to work.

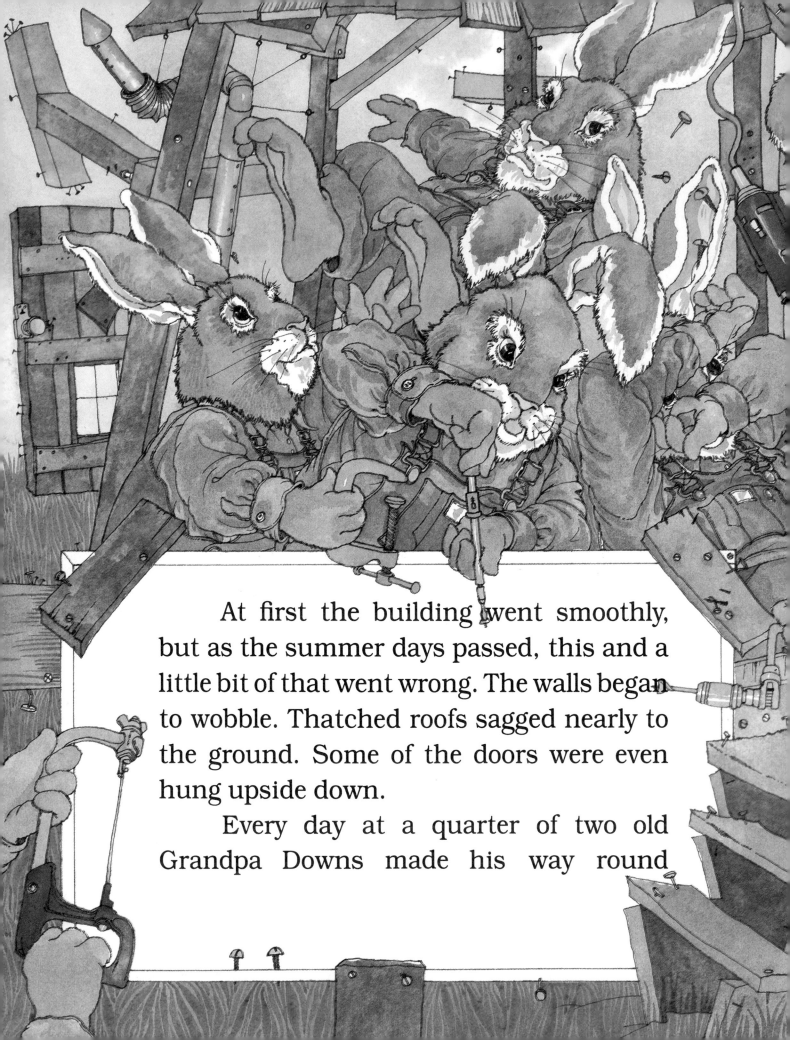

At first the building went smoothly, but as the summer days passed, this and a little bit of that went wrong. The walls began to wobble. Thatched roofs sagged nearly to the ground. Some of the doors were even hung upside down.

Every day at a quarter of two old Grandpa Downs made his way round

the site and offered suggestions on how to make things right. "When I was a boy, in the good old days, we would have done this differently."

But the builder bunnies just shooed him away, for after all, Grandpa Downs was one of the silvered hares and everyone knows how the olden golden ones liked to babble on about the good old days.

Knowing that they weren't wanted, the older rabbits wandered about. They looked at the flowers that bloomed, they tasted the sweet berries that grew, but there was nothing to do and they were terribly bored.

Mostly they stood about warming themselves in the sun, watching the buildings being built. They would shake their silvered heads and say, "Tsk, tsk, tsk! It will never work. It never will!"

But the younger rabbits ignored them, and continued to build in the meadow.

Now, as it always was in the Land of Barely There in the latter part of summer, the winds blew mightily from the mountains. The wind at first began to whisper through the pines a gentle warning, whipping wisps of cloud about the mountain. But the clouds got bigger and bigger and blacker and blacker.

The old silvered hares, as they sat warming in a patch of sunlight, stopped

and sniffed at the wind.

"Oh, oh," said Grandma Downs. "It's a storm, a mighty storm from the mountains of Barely There!" Filled with wisdom of storms long past and fear for the future, they all rushed to the meadow to warn the others.

With scarves and shawls flapping, they hopped into the meadow shouting, "Run for the burrows! Run for the burrows! There comes a mighty mountain storm."

As the worker bunnies dropped their tools and turned to run, Derby shouted, "Stop, you fools! They are warning of the olden days and wish us only to go back to the burrows."

All the worker bunnies warily looked at the silvered hares but returned to their work.

"But, but," stuttered Grandpa Downs. "When I was a boy these storms were . . ."

Derby whirled, and in a challenging voice said, "Listen old hare, when you were a

boy was a long time ago, and we are a lot smarter now. Go hide in your dank, dark burrow. Hide in the candle's flicker. We're not afraid of a silly summer storm." And with that he stomped back to work.

With a tear trickling down his graying cheek, Grandpa Downs hopped back to the burrows where the older rabbits were protecting themselves against the storm.

In the meadow, Derby called to his friends who were standing around looking just a bit nervous. "Look about; although a gentle breeze does blow, the sun still shines. Don't listen to those old fools. Come back to work!"

Satisfied with Derby's bravado, all the bunnies went back to work. But still the darkening clouds gathered round the meadow and the wind began to whip and blow.

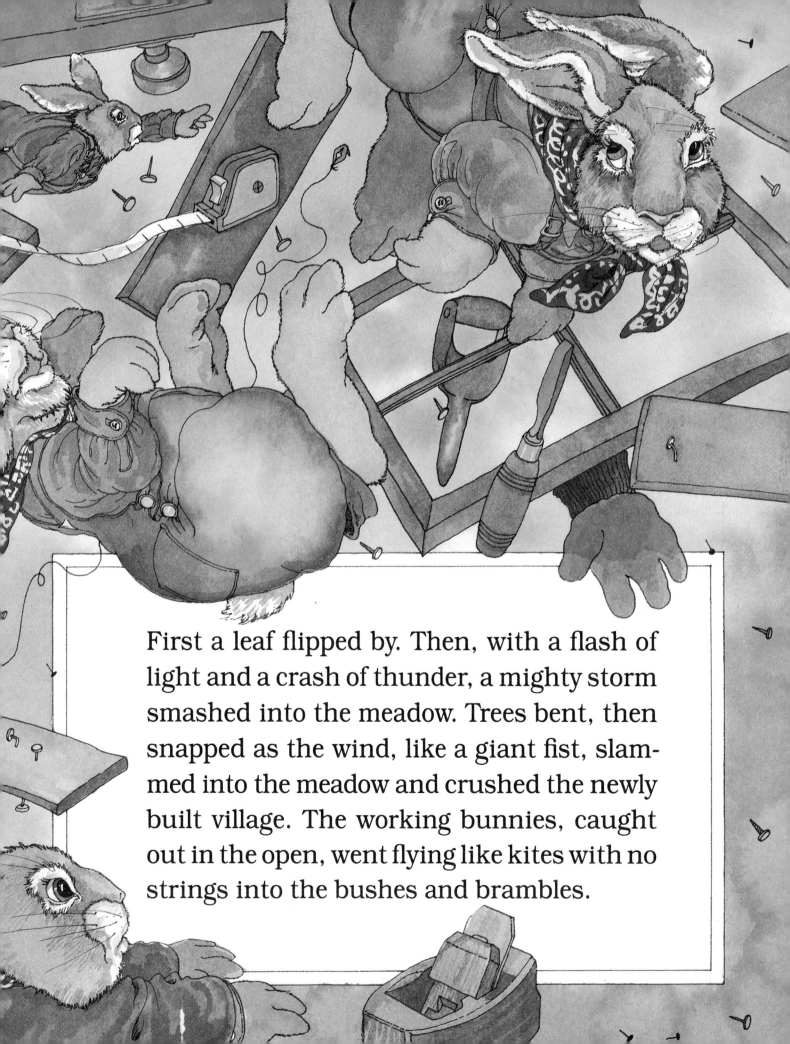

First a leaf flipped by. Then, with a flash of light and a crash of thunder, a mighty storm smashed into the meadow. Trees bent, then snapped as the wind, like a giant fist, slammed into the meadow and crushed the newly built village. The working bunnies, caught out in the open, went flying like kites with no strings into the bushes and brambles.

The storm raged for a only a moment, and then, like a wickless candle, sputtered out. Once again the meadow was bathed in sunlight. But the meadow had changed! The buildings were all blown down and the worker bunnies were sprawled in the trees.

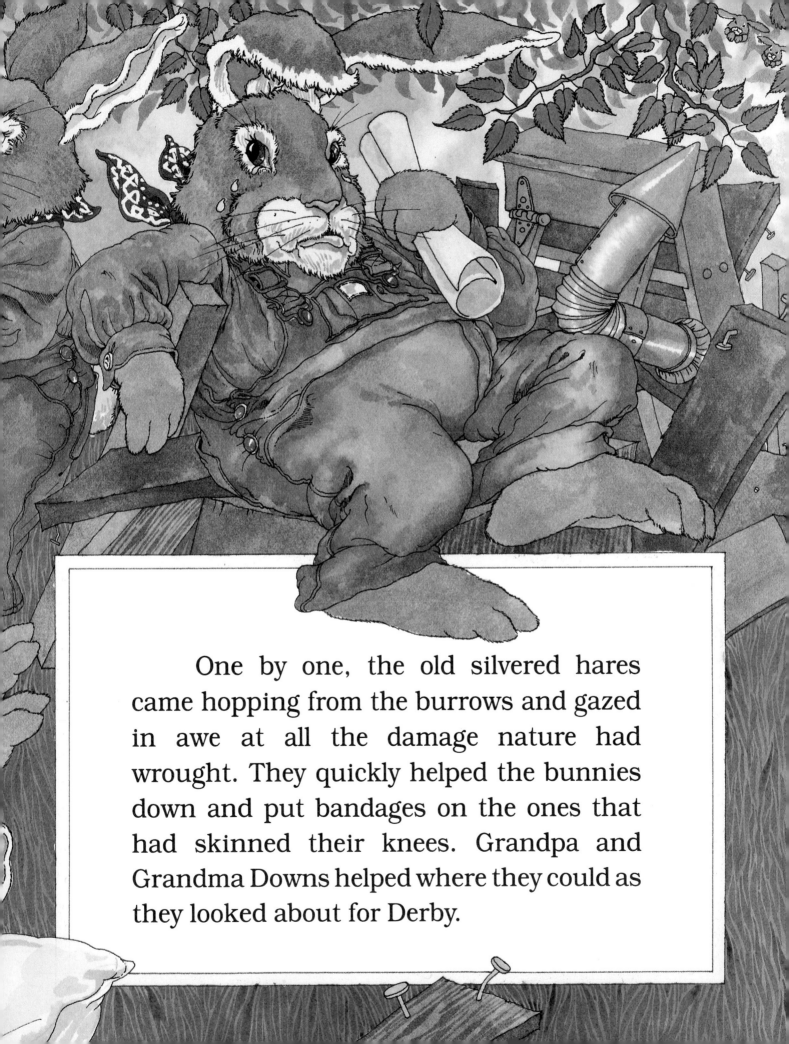

One by one, the old silvered hares came hopping from the burrows and gazed in awe at all the damage nature had wrought. They quickly helped the bunnies down and put bandages on the ones that had skinned their knees. Grandpa and Grandma Downs helped where they could as they looked about for Derby.

They finally found him sitting on a pile of rubble shaking his head in disbelief. They rushed to his side and happily hugged him, filled with joy that he was safe. Like a child, Derby openly wept on Grandpa's furry shoulder.

"Don't cry, Derby," consoled Grandma and Grandpa. "No one was seriously hurt, and all will be well in the meadow."

"But I didn't listen to your warnings. I didn't listen to your advice about building in the meadow, and I didn't listen when you warned about the storm."

Grandpa held Derby Downs very close and said in his olden golden voice, "There were others before you who didn't heed warnings. Remember, I told you the story of the good old days and of a silly rabbit who wished to build in the meadow. Well, that silly rabbit was me, and I learned as you shall learn that you can gain wisdom from any mistake."

Thus, Derby and the other bunnies learned from the past and prospered in the meadows as they improved the burrows that were built below the ground. In the evenings, as the flickering fire caused shadows to dance, they listened in wonder as the silvered hares spoke wisely of the good old days . . . in the Land of Barely There.

Other books
in this series

Fiddler
Gossamer
Hannah & Hickory
Ira Wordworthy
Persimmony
Shadow Chaser
T.J. Flopp